TEA AT THE LITTLE BIG TOP

by James Driscoll
Illustrated by Rob Lee

Storm Publishing

Charlie had spent most of the morning cleaning his house

Charlie has been a circus clown all of his life and that is the reason he lives in a house that looks like a circus tent.

Circus tents are called Big Tops but Charlie's house is quit small so he calls it The Little Big Top.

The inside of The Little Big Top is as clean as a new pin. There isn't any carpet on the floor because Charlie prefers sawdust just like a real circus ring.

The large round table with five red stars painted on the top was once a stand the big elephants used when they did their tricks. The four smaller stands make very good stools and hanging from the roof is a trapeze with a glittering gold bar.

Charlie had set the table for tea.

There were two plates with sandwiches cut into triangles. On one plate were cucumber sandwiches and on the other tomato sandwiches.

The cake stand was full of lovely chocolate cakes covered in thick icing with little cream whirls on top. Four pretty tea cups, saucers and plates were placed on each star ready for tea.

"My goodness, just look at the time," said Charlie as he put the milk jug and sugar bowl on the table.

Charlie's clock has a funny clown's face and when the time comes to strike each hour the clown's hat lifts off his head and a loud clash of cymbals can be heard.

CRASH! CRASH! CRASH!

"Three o'clock, they'll be here any moment," said Charlie standing in front of the mirror, straightening his hat.

Charlie had invited Margot, Trampy and Sergeant Major to tea. Outside the entrance to The Little Big Top is a very large car horn with a big rubber ball at one end. A small notice reads "Press Twice", so Trampy squeezed the rubber ball twice. HONK! HONK!

"I HAVE NEVER SEEN SUCH A STUPID DOOR BELL IN ALL MY LIFE. NOTHING BUT A NUISANCE TO PEOPLE. SHOULD BE REPORTED," said Sergeant Major, crossly.

"Now just a moment Sergeant Major. Charlie has been very kind to invite us for tea, so I want you to promise me that you are going to be nice to him. No comments about his door horn. Is that a promise? Well?" asked Trampy, looking very serious indeed.

"VERY WELL, I PROMISE," said Sergeant Major shrugging his shoulders.

Charlie opened the flaps of The Little Big Top and welcomed them all to tea.

Margot had brought Charlie a lovely bunch of flowers picked from her garden. Charlie took a beautiful red rose from the bunch and put it in his buttonhole.

"Please come and sit down, the kettle has just boiled. I will go and make the tea," said Charlie.

He was soon back carrying the funniest teapot that you have ever seen. The teapot had four spouts. Margot and Trampy laughed and laughed. Sergeant Major looked quite confused by its strange shape.

"Oh Charlie, what sort of teapot is that?" asked Margot still laughing.

"This is called a tea for four teapot, designed by a very funny and very clever clown, namely me," explained Charlie. He then placed the cups together and to everyone's amazement poured four cups of tea all at the same time not spilling a drop.

"Bravo! That is the cleverest teapot that I have ever seen," said Trampy eating a delicious chocolate cake.

They had soon eaten the lovely sandwiches and cakes Charlie had made for them. "That was a very nice tea Charlie. Thank you so much from all of us," said Margot.

"The time has come to show you my latest trick," announced Charlie. "Sergeant Major, can I borrow your hat for a few minutes?"

"CERTAINLY NOT! HER MAJESTY'S ARMY UNIFORM IS NOT TO BE USED BY CLOWNS," said Sergeant Major, shaking his head.

"Oh, please do, Sergeant Major. Don't be a spoilsport," pleaded Margot fluttering her long eyelashes at him.

Sergeant Major couldn't say no to Margot and very reluctantly passed his hat to Charlie.

Charlie held Sergeant Major's hat in one hand and picked up the tea for four teapot in the other. Then to everyone's surprise he poured tea into the hat. Sergeant Major was speechless.

Soon the teapot was empty.

Charlie threw the hat high into the air. Margot, Trampy and Sergeant Major all ducked thinking that they were about to get very wet.

As the hat turned in the air a shower of sparkling stars fell from it but not a single drop of tea.

The hat landed in the middle of the table completely dry and looking as good as new.

They cheered and cheered. Even Sergeant Major clapped.

Tea at The Little Big Top was always exciting.